Grunge Music

There's music everywhere in this celebration of songs.

Story by:
Ken Forsse

Illustrated by:
David High
Russell Hicks
Rennie Rau
Theresa Mazurek
Allyn Conley/Gorniak

WORLDS OF WONDER™

Grubby™   Newton Gimmick™   Princess Aruzia™   Leota™   Wooly What's-It™

Prince Arin™   Fobs™

Page 1

"Do the Grunge"

It's easy to do. You just get up and go.

"There's Rhythm Everywhere"

"The Octopede Shuffle"

"Syncopation Celebration"

Get in tune with a vibration of a positive kind.

"Surfin' Grundo"

Maybe we can join 'em and go surfin' now and then.